Isabelle's Wish

Isabelle's Wish

Cara D. Brown

iUniverse, Inc.
Bloomington

ISABELLE'S WISH

iUniverse books may be ordered through booksellers or by contacting:

iUniverse
1663 Liberty Drive
Bloomington, IN 47403
www.iuniverse.com
1-800-Authors (1-800-288-4677)

ISBN: 978-1-4759-7421-8 (sc)
ISBN: 978-1-4759-7422-5 (ebk)

Library of Congress Control Number: 2013901872

Printed in the United States of America

iUniverse rev. date: 02/15/2013

Chapter 1

School's Out

Isabelle Brandy Stevens
7 years old

Zachary Bailey Stevens
9 years old
Isabelle's older brother

In Fairfax, Virginia, on a Friday at 3:30 p.m. in the spring of 2014, Zachary and Isabelle are about to get out of school. Zachary is nine years old and in the fourth grade, and his sister, Isabelle, is seven years old and in the second grade. They both go to the same school, Piney Branch Elementary. Once school ends, the bell rings at Piney Branch Elementary at 3:30 p.m. Isabelle and Zachary begin walking home together. Isabelle says," Let's go home a different way." Zachary sighs "Isabelle let's just go home the normal way" but Isabelle takes off down Springfield Court. Zachary runs after her as they approach Lonetree Way, Isabelle notices the haunted house on the corner.

Isabelle looks at Zachary and says, "Look there's the haunted house! I dare you to knock on the door and go inside."

Zachary says, "No, I don't want to. Mom is waiting for us at home."

Isabelle ignores him and runs up toward the house. Zachary rolls his eyes and sighs and then starts to run after her. Isabelle reaches the haunted house's front door and knocks. She calls out, "Hello is anybody home?"

Chapter 2

What Are You Doing?

The door opens a little, but nobody seems to be there. Isabelle pushes the door open farther and goes inside. Isabelle walks around the house and finds a woman in the study sitting in a chair. The back of the chair is facing the door, but the chair slowly begins to swivel around to face Isabelle. The woman is middle-aged and looks a lot like Isabelle's mother but with longer hair.

The woman says, "Well, hello. I've been waiting for you."

Isabelle's mouth drops open in surprise, and she says, "Mom, is that you?"

Zachary comes running into the study and says, "Isabelle, what are you doing? Mom is waiting." Zachary sees the middle-aged woman talking to Isabelle and wonders, *what is going on here?*

The woman continues talking to Isabelle. "No, I am not your mother. My name is Gabriella, and I know your mom very well. I am here to grant you your wish."

Isabelle asks, "What wish?"

Gabriella responds, "The wish that you have been praying for for three years."

Zachary asks Isabelle, "What have you done?"

Isabelle looks at Zachary with confusion in her eyes. Suddenly, Zachary and Isabelle begin to feel an earthquake coming on. Zachary and Isabelle dive under the table and cling to each other until the shaking stops. Once the earthquake is over, Zachary and Isabelle open their eyes. Everything around them looks different, and Gabriella is nowhere to be found. Zachary and Isabelle look at each other and say . . .

Gabriella

Chapter 3

Where Are We?

Mikey

Evan Collins

Earl Collins

The Hungry Bear

"Where are we?" Zachary and Isabelle have entered a time warp. They have been transported back sixty-six million years ago to a jungle with vines and huge ferns with lots of green grass and dinosaurs.

Zachary asks Isabelle, "What is going on here? What is your wish?"

Isabelle begins to tell him her wish but stops when she sees a dinosaur running toward them. Zachary starts to run away from the dinosaur, but Isabelle is not afraid. She walks closer to the dinosaur and pets him.

She tells the dinosaur, "Hello, Mikey; I will call you Mikey." Mikey likes Isabelle, and they become fast friends. Just at that moment, Zachary sees two boys approaching them. They are the evil twin brothers, Evan and Earl Collins, who try to scare everybody they see away from their territory.

The twins speak at the same time. "What do you think you are doing here? You do not belong here. This place is not big enough for all of us! We can't let you stay here."

Just as they rush toward Zachary and Isabelle, Gabriella reappears. She tells the Collins boys, "Don't you dare. Leave these kids alone." The evil twins are afraid of Gabriella, which makes them not so scary after all.

They slink away and mutter to Zachary and Isabelle, "This is not over."

Gabriella tells Isabelle, "You must hurry, my dear, and find common ground."

"Common ground, what do you mean?" Isabelle asks.

Gabriella disappears into thin air before she can respond, and Zachary and Isabelle are left confused. Meanwhile, the evil twins are waiting in the bushes. Once they see that Gabriella is gone, they come back to chase Zachary and Isabelle away. Zachary and Isabelle see the evil twins and begin to run toward a dark cave. They run inside the cave, and the only thing they can see are big, intense, and scary eyes staring at them. Scared, Zachary and Isabelle stare back, they hear a hungry bear.

Chapter 4

What Is Your Wish?

Zachary and Isabelle scream and take off running toward the other end of the cave. It's a bear! The hungry bear licks his lips as if Zachary and Isabelle were his lunch. As Zachary and Isabelle escape the cave, Mikey appears. Zachary and Isabelle climb onto his back and Mikey starts running really fast. Just as the bear is gaining on them, Mikey sprouts wings and flies off into the sunset.

Once they are safely away from the evil twins and the hungry bear, Mikey glides down and softly lands. Zachary and Isabelle get off his back.

Zachary and Isabelle both say, "Thanks, Mikey, for the ride." Then Mikey walks over to where Gabriella is.

Gabriella says to Isabelle, "You are almost there, honey. Good luck." Then Gabriella climbs on Mikey's back, and she and Mikey ride off into the evening sky.

Zachary asks Isabelle, "Okay, what is your wish?"

Isabelle says . . .

Chapter 5

Home, Sweet Home!

"Gabby" Elizabeth Stevens
Mom

Michael Brandon Stevens
Dad

"My wish is . . . ah, well, I wish . . . that you liked me. Sometimes I feel like you are mad at me all the time and that you don't like me. I want us to be friends."

Zachary rolls his eyes at her and says, "Of course we're friends. You're my sister." Zachary tells Isabelle that he l—l—loves her. Isabelle smiles and tells Zachary that she loves him too. Then she leans over to kiss him on the cheek. Zachary leans backward and cringes.

"Agh," he cries while she kisses him. Just at that moment, an earthquake happens again, and Zachary and Isabelle are back in front of Piney Branch Elementary, the bell rings at 3:30 p.m. Zachary says, "Can we go home the normal way this time?" Isabelle says, "Okay." Zachary and Isabelle trudge home tired and hungry as if several hours have gone by, when they walk into the front door of their house, the clock on the wall says it is 4:00p.m. Their mom, Gabby and their dad, Michael are in the kitchen fixing dinner.

Their mom says, "Well, hello. I've been waiting for you. You are usually back home before now. You kids look kind of droopy. I think you need more excitement at school."

Zachary and Isabelle look at each other and laugh.

"What's so funny?" their mom asks.

The End

Printed in the United States
By Bookmasters